CROSSING THE LINES

A VAMPIRE BOOK CLUB PREQUEL

NANCY WARREN

ISBN: ebook 978-1-990210-23-5

ISBN: print 978-1-998239-11-5

Ambleside Publishing

INTRODUCTION

Crossing the Lines

Seattle witch Quinn Callahan knew she wasn't supposed to mess with death. Now, the Grim Reaper's turned up at her book club and he's not there for the gossip and the cheese plate.

In this prequel to *The Vampire Book Club* series of paranormal cozy mysteries, learn how Quinn first met the gorgeous Irish vampire Lochlan Balfour and joined forces.

"This prequel has definitely set the scene for a fantastic read. I can't recommend Nancy's books high enough! Unput-downable!!!" *****

If you haven't met Rafe Crosyer yet, he's the gorgeous, sexy vampire in *The Vampire Knitting Club* series. You can get his origin story free when you join Nancy's no-spam newsletter at NancyWarrenAuthor.com.

Come join Nancy in her private Facebook group where we talk about books, knitting, pets and life. www.facebook.com/groups/NancyWarrenKnitwits

CROSSING THE LINES

CHAPTER 1

I knew tangling with Death was a bad idea.

I'd been a practicing witch all my adult life, so I didn't mess with powerful dark magic lightly. But when my best friend and former husband was dying and wanted so badly to stay, I let my emotions get the better of my judgment.

Yes. Ex-husband. Truth was, we never should have married. We were destined to be friends. And we were. After our marriage ended, he found the perfect woman for him and, strange as it may sound, the three of us were close. Their two girls grew up calling me Auntie Quinn. So, when I interfered with Death, maybe I wasn't just trying to save my ex. I was trying to keep their dad around for two girls I loved as though they were my own.

Being a witch has certain responsibilities that come with the vocation. The first rule is Do No Harm. There's another lesser known rule that basically says don't mess with Death. However, in a moment of weakness, and genuinely trying to do a good thing, I cast a spell that was both extremely powerful and very dangerous. It almost surprised me when it worked. My ex went into remission from the cancer that was eating his body. We all celebrated, though there was an edge of fear to my happiness because I knew that somewhere along the line I was going to have to pay.

Sadly, the party was short-lived. Yes, his remission gave him more quality hours with his beloved wife and daughters, but in the end, he still died, and they still mourned.

And I waited.

Nothing happened for a few months. I thought I'd freaked out for nothing. And then one night I was sitting reading my novel for book club. It was one of those women's journey type novels that was harrowing to read, and halfway through the story I was pretty sure it wasn't going to end well for anybody. I was already depressed enough. I'd lost my ex-husband, who'd been one of my best friends, and I watched helplessly as his wife and girls struggled with their grief. The last thing I needed was a depressing reminder that sometimes life really blows.

I put the book down, stood up and stretched. Scanned my bookshelves, looking for a light read where everything would turn out all right in the end.

My fingers skimmed through the various titles on my bookshelves. It was an eclectic mix, everything from romance and thrillers to cookbooks, books on herbs and oils and fragrances, all useful in my craft. And then my fingertips touched my grimoire. At forty-five years old, I was accustomed to the way power can surprise you. But I saw sparks and pulled my hand away as it felt like my fingertips were burning. I shuddered, knowing *that* spell was in there. The Death Spell, as I now called it.

If it wasn't an old and fascinating grimoire, I'd have been

tempted to throw the spell book away. Just touching the dark blue leather binding reminded me of what I'd done. I no longer felt like reading. I'd run myself a hot bath and chuck in some of the special oil I made that was both therapeutic and magical. A bath might help relax me out of this jittery mood.

I turned from the bookcase and jumped about a mile in the air, a scream catching in my throat.

There was a strange man standing there. Right in the living room of my Seattle home.

"Who are you?" Not the most original response, perhaps, but it's surprising how that is the first thing you think when there's a strange guy standing in your living room.

He didn't look threatening or dangerous. He had a pleasant face, short, dark hair, and wore black slacks, black shoes, a white shirt, and a blazer with no tie. In his right hand he carried a briefcase. He looked like an accountant or a lawyer who'd accidentally wandered into my living room.

Except that I kept my doors locked.

"I'm Arthur," he said.

I didn't have weapons in the house, but I did have powers, so I wasn't terrified as much as I was startled. "What are you doing in my house, Arthur?"

He smiled a little at that. "I think you know."

Okay, I was getting a bad feeling about this in the pit of my stomach. I thought maybe I did know why he was here, but I wasn't going to jump right in and ask if he was Death or some minor minion in Death's employ. "I really don't."

"I'm a debt collector."

"My bills are all paid up."

He shook his head at that. "Not the one I'm thinking of.

You changed a man's fate. It's against the rules of both your world and mine. Gregory Chambers was destined to die at a certain date and time." He stopped and opened his briefcase. Inside it was a tablet that looked electronic but probably wasn't. He gazed down at it for a second. "Thanks to your interference, his death was deferred by sixty-one days." He glanced up at me as though I might care to argue with his facts.

I drew in a breath and straightened my spine so that I reached my full height. "A few weeks didn't really change anything." I wasn't going to admit that I had delayed his death, but I wasn't going to lie to a guy who had everybody's life and death on this magical tablet. That would be stupid.

"But you don't know all the things that changed because of your interference. My boss is very displeased and needs to make an example of you. I'm here to take your life."

I'd expected something, but not this. I stared at him. "You're as funny as a heart attack."

He put his head back and forth like an Italian deciding between two types of pasta. "I was thinking brain aneurysm, but sure. Heart attack works."

So not what I'd meant. "Look. Why don't you let me talk to your boss? We can work this out. I've learned my lesson. I promise I won't do it again."

He looked at me as though I was a few books short of a library. "You will be meeting my boss. You have to die first."

"Right. That's the part I'm not really comfortable with. I have a better idea. Why don't you carry my message back to your boss and ask for a second chance?"

His lips curved slightly in a smile that was terrifying because it was so bland. "Death doesn't give second chances."

"There's a first time for everything!" I said in my cheeriest voice.

"I'm sorry, Quinn Callaghan. Your timeline has been adjusted. Forty-five years on this earth is what you've been given. But don't worry, I'll see you again soon."

He raised his hand and stepped towards me and I didn't even think about it. Before he could burst a blood vessel in my brain, I yelled, "No!" in my loudest voice, at the same time pushing my right hand forward and calling on all my power to counter whatever he was throwing at me. I had no idea if I had the strength and power to beat back one of Death's messengers, but I didn't have anything to lose.

My hand burned as though it was on fire. It was like that zing I'd had when I'd touched my grimoire, only a million times more powerful. The pain was so great tears were pouring from my eyes, but I couldn't hold off. There was a moment when my power clashed with his and it was like a huge explosion in the middle of my living room. All the lights went out. And there was a rumble like a tiny earthquake.

When it was over, I was on the floor. I didn't even know how I'd ended up there. And I was alone.

CHAPTER 2

I glanced around, but apart from a slight smell of burning, there was no indication Arthur had ever been there. I could have imagined it except that all the fingernails on my right hand were singed black.

I didn't waste as much as a minute. I pulled out every protection spell I knew and traced the perimeter of my house, especially the windowsills and the door jambs, with a powerful mixture of salt and magic that was supposed to keep evil at bay.

Not that Death was evil, but we were definitely not on good terms right now.

I called in sick to the law firm where I worked as a librarian and remained home for two days.

Two days that equaled forty-eight hours when I was constantly on edge and looking over my shoulder. Then, at some point, I realized I might as well be dead if I was going to wall myself up in my house as though it were a coffin. I'd sent a message back to Death and maybe that was all I needed to do.

I could live my life, whatever was left of it, a free woman.

At least I hoped so. Just in case Arthur had plans to finish what he'd started, I drove to Fremont to my good friend and the head of our coven, Diana List. Diana lived in a yellow cottage with a vibrant front garden of herbs, veggies, and flowers mixed together in a riot of scent and color. She opened her door in a swish of flowing black linen dress accented with silver jewelry. Even her hair was silver and hung loose in soft curls. I felt downright corporate in blue slacks and a white sweater.

"You'd better come in." Wow. Diana wasn't as friendly as she normally was. In fact, she was downright standoffish. Obviously, I knew she was a powerful witch, but I'd never felt it the way I did that afternoon. Her living room was a clutter of crystals, candles, books, and mismatched furniture. I could smell the herbs I knew were drying in her kitchen.

She didn't offer me a seat so I remained standing. I pretended not to notice her coldness and related what had happened from the moment I'd cast that spell to save Greg to today. "I need your help, Di. Extra protection. Whatever you've got."

"I'd sensed something was wrong," she said, looking at me as though she were very disappointed in me. "But I didn't imagine this. Quinn, what were you thinking? You defied Death?"

When she put it that way it did sound like I'd done a supremely stupid thing. I tried to explain that I hadn't thought, I'd gone with emotion. But she didn't care about my excuses.

"Dangerous, foolish, calamitous witch," she said to me. "You've brought Death among us. We have very clear rules.

Death has his domain. We have ours. Never, never do we interfere with his work. And now you have. You've opened the portal between our two worlds."

"Oh, come on. You're being a bit dramatic, aren't you? Death comes among us every day. Go read the obituaries."

She leveled a cold gaze my way. "That's not the same, and you know it."

"All right. Look, I screwed up, I admit it, but I really don't think it's a crime punishable by my death. What am I going to do?"

"I don't know. I've never been in this situation before. Every witch I've ever known had the sense to stay away from this kind of trouble."

I told her about how I'd used my magic to sweep Arthur out of my house. "All I need is something that will protect me from him. Come on, that's not using dark magic. Protection is good. I'm one of your sisters and a good friend—"

She held up a finger and shook it at me. "Don't you say I owe you. Don't you say those words. Because I don't. The minute you dabbled in something so dangerous without even talking to me about it first, you negated our friendship."

Wow. That was harsh. I took a step back feeling cold inside and broken. I turned to go and her voice called me back.

"Wait." I turned and saw her looking deeply troubled. "Come here."

I went closer. She took a silver bracelet off her left wrist and reached for my hand.

I pulled back. "I can't take this. It's your protection charm."

"It's the strongest thing I have. And you need it a lot more than I do." Then she shook her head. "Follow me."

She led me upstairs to the converted attic in her house that was her magic room. A circle of black candles was already waiting. I glanced at her.

"You knew I was coming."

"I had a vision."

"I'm sorry."

"Go stand in the middle of the circle," she said, as though she was sending me to the time-out chair.

I hung my head and did as she asked. She joined me and then cast the circle, and as she did so the flames of the candles sprang instantly to life. She reached for my hand and when her fingers circled the silver bracelet around my wrist, I felt power pulsing through my veins, and instantly I pictured a wall of energy surrounding me.

Diana closed her eyes and breathed deeply. I did the same. Her voice was deep and rich.

"Spirits of the air, earth, fire, and water,
We call on you to help this unruly daughter,
Shield her from the evil and the dark
Anywhere she may embark.
So we will, so mote it be."

I heard a sound like rushing wind and opened my eyes to see the candles all blow out at once. I shivered with the sudden cold. "Did you do that?" I asked in a small voice.

Diana turned to me. "No."

Oh, that could not be good.

As I was leaving her house, Diana said, "This isn't the end of it, Quinn. I have to take this to the next level."

When did the supernatural world become so bureaucratic? Death was sending guys around with briefcases and computer tablets, and my coven sister was talking about elevating my mistake to a higher level. Exactly the way we handled disciplinary actions at my law firm. No doubt the Witches' Council had their own investigatory and disciplinary branches. Internal affairs for witches. That was just what I needed.

Still, she was only doing her job, so I nodded.

"Blessed be," she said as I left.

Those words had never meant more. I turned back to her. "Blessed be," I echoed.

BACK OUT ON the street it was raining. Which was not news in Seattle. I didn't have an umbrella. I didn't own one. Never saw the point. I'd get wet. I'd dry out. It was easier than trying to remember where I'd put umbrellas, and what did you do with wet ones, anyway?

I got back in my car and returned to my house in Capitol Hill.

At least in the forty-eight hours I'd been walled up at home, I'd finished the book club book. We were meeting that night at Jane Eddington's house. Jane lived with her husband Ronald on Queen Anne Hill in a beautiful, old mansion.

She was also the one who usually chose the books. Jane was a retired lit professor from the University of Washington. She and her former co-worker, Frances Sheehy, were the most intellectual among us. Jane had a great house and loved to cook so we let her push morose morality tales on us. Jane had been Frances's boss as department head and it was funny how she still exerted authority over her. Frances often tried to suggest a lighter book, as we all did, but Jane usually got her way. "Happy endings are fine for fluffy, meaningless novels," she'd say, as though we were her students, "but we learn so much more delving into the darkest parts of the human psyche." And so we'd end up reading yet another harrowing tale of death, despair, and madness.

The best part of book club was the food. None of us would admit we were competitive, but what had started out as a simple potluck where somebody might bring a cheese plate and somebody else might bake a batch of brownies had turned into an evening of gourmet delights. I didn't bother to eat dinner before I went.

With forty-eight hours at home, not only had I read the book, I'd searched Epicurious for a daring finger food and discovered Goat Cheese Croquettes with Spiced Membrillo. Membrillo turned out to be quince paste and I spent the better part of a day getting the recipe right. Then I put my croquettes on a yellow and blue hand-potted plate. I casually placed my contribution on the walnut dining table. Kanako, a graphic artist, had brought her homemade sushi. Maya, a doctor, wowed us with polenta made with fontina cheese and wild mushrooms she'd harvested herself—I am not kidding. The last to arrive, dripping rain and apologies, was Kimberlee. She was in her twenties and Jane's protegée. She was working on her PhD in literature and would one day, no doubt, follow in Jane's footsteps.

We settled in Jane's living room. I sat in one of the gold

velvet chairs among priceless antiques carefully set on an Aubusson rug. Crystal lamps lit the room.

All of us drank wine except Jane, who only ever drank scotch from a Waterford decanter that sat on a sideboard among her various awards and photographs.

"Before we begin, let's choose the next novel we'll read," Jane said. She looked at us all over the top of her reading glasses. "Nominations?"

I no longer bothered suggesting books. I'd been shot down too many times. Kimberlee was too awed by Jane to ever suggest a novel, though she must read hundreds of them. Kanako suggested a new novel by an Indian author. "The New York Times called it 'life-affirming and ground-breaking.'"

Jane wrinkled her nose. "It's a translation."

Frances reached into her bag and pulled out a hardback with a beautiful cover. I perked up as the colors weren't variations of gray and black. "I'd like to suggest Pillary Road. A first novel by a young woman who came to this country as a refugee and writes about women triumphing over adversity. It's one of the best novels I've read in a decade and it's nominated for a National Book Award."

Jane held out her hand and Frances gave her the novel. Jane scanned the back cover copy and then opened the cover and glanced at the first page. I think we all held our breath, hoping we might be able to read a novel that held out some hope for the human condition. After a minute, Jane wrinkled her nose. "Pedestrian prose," she stated, handing the book back.

Then she lifted a novel from the table beside her. Darker than Death was the title and its cover was, sure enough, a study of black and gray. I felt depressed just looking at it. "Written from the perspective of a supposedly insane woman in Victorian London, this novel is a study in betrayal and madness." She glanced around at us all once more. "I took the liberty of ordering copies for each of us."

End of discussion.

We paused to refill our wine glasses and dive into discussing this week's depressathon. I tried to think of puppies and babies laughing when the discussion got too dark.

I did throw in a couple of comments so they'd know I'd read the book. I also enjoyed the perspective each woman brought to her reading and I genuinely liked these women, but it was still a relief when we took a food break.

Jane's husband Ronald Eddington was a retired history professor and acted as server and wine steward at these gatherings. He handed me a china plate and a linen napkin wrapped around sterling cutlery and I helped myself to the goodies. "Ronald, did you make the salad?"

"I did. Kale with hazelnuts and cranberry."

"Yum. You should join our book club. You're here anyway."

His chuckle was as dry and colorless as he was. "Novels are Jane's domain. It's always been that way." I got the feeling he was forbidden to join us.

We settled back down with our food and Ronald topped up glasses. I asked Kanako about a protest she was involved in to save some neighborhood trees from a developer.

Frances and Maya were chatting about a play they'd both seen, and Jane was asking Kimberlee about her thesis.

Suddenly, Jane made the strangest sound. Something

resembling a cat with a furball. She stood up looking very surprised, her eyes opened wide.

"Jane, what's wrong?" Kimberlee asked.

I half rose wondering if she was choking. She staggered forward a couple of paces and then collapsed to the floor.

Maya was instantly on her knees by Jane's side. "Call 911," she yelled. Kanako was already making the call and swiftly described what had happened and gave the address.

"Ambulance is on its way," she said.

But it was too late.

I knew it before Maya sat back on her heels and shook her head. I'd sensed it. Jane was gone.

"What's wrong with her?" Frances asked, her hands at her chest.

"She's dead," Maya said.

"What did she die of?" Kimberlee asked, her voice rising. "She was just sitting here a few minutes ago talking to me about my thesis supervisor. She was fine."

The doctor shook her head. "We'll know more when we get her to hospital. My guess is a brain aneurysm."

CHAPTER 3

*A*fter the body had been removed and a young police officer had attended and briefly asked us all what we'd seen, and received identical stories from each of us, he took all our names and contact information and we were allowed to leave. Ronald looked shell-shocked and even though Frances and Maya both offered to stay with him, he shook his head. "I've got a sister. I'll call her."

We all left together, still expressing our shock and sympathy. Kanako turned back. "In my state I forgot my phone." She made a helpless gesture. "We'll talk soon." And she retraced her steps.

I was filled not only with horror but guilt. My heart was pounding a million miles a minute and, while I'd never been a big fan of Death, right now I had a huge hate on for him.

I drove straight back to my house, frantic. A brain aneurysm? Really? A brain aneurysm?

My keys rattled in my hand as I unlocked my front door. I was so upset. Usually I liked living alone, but right now I wished I had somebody to come home to. Even a cat. I'd had familiars over the years, but the last one hadn't stayed and I had yet to find my new one. Or, realistically, it would find me. In my experience, they always did.

I wished it would find me now. Familiars weren't always cats. I would embrace a hedgehog, a porcupine, a rat if it would give me some kind of comfort.

I paced up and down for a few minutes and then yelled, "Arthur!"

Nothing.

"Arthur, I bet you can hear me. I know you're still around. Show yourself, I command you."

Could I command Death's minion? I didn't know. However, I had a huge mad on and a lot of focus. I waited for him to appear in the middle of my living room like he had last time, and instead there was a knock on the door.

I looked through my peephole and there was Arthur, looking as though he might be here to fix my computer or discuss my insurance needs. I flung open the door. "You're so polite all of a sudden?"

He indicated the trail of salt across the bottom of the entranceway. It was the first bit of cheer I'd experienced all evening. So, my protection spell worked. Good. I certainly wasn't going to invite him to step over the threshold. Instead I stood there, arms wrapped around my waist, glaring. "What the hell are you trying to do to me?"

He looked slightly taken aback. "I beg your pardon?"

"You killed a woman in my book club with a brain aneurysm. What kind of message are you trying to send me? Are you going to kill all my friends until I agree to sacrifice myself to you?"

He blinked and his expression grew wary. "I'm not aware of what you're talking about."

I moved my arms from around my waist and propped my hands on my hips.

"Don't play games with me. Why did you kill that woman? What did Jane Eddington ever do to you?"

He shook his head. "I'm really not following you."

With exaggerated patience, I said, "Jane Eddington. Tonight, at book club on Queen Anne Hill. Right in front of me, she fell down dead from a brain aneurysm. Sound familiar?"

He opened his ever handy briefcase and pulled out that weird tablet. A little tapping of his fingers and he looked up at me. "I had nothing to do with that."

I seriously wanted to believe him, but the coincidence was too great. "You told me you were going to kill me with a brain aneurysm but I was able to get you out of my house by magic. Three days later I go to my book club meeting and a perfectly healthy woman falls down in front of me, dead from a brain aneurysm. And you're telling me this is pure coincidence?"

Much as I wanted to believe him, it was a stretch.

He was gazing down at his tablet and then looked up at me with a puzzled expression. "Why do you think she died of a brain aneurysm?"

I shrugged. "Because the doctor said it was the most likely cause of death. Why?"

He assumed an expression of innocence. "No reason."

"Come on. You work for Death. You must know what the woman died of."

"But I am not at liberty to share that information with mortals."

"You're a pain in my ass, do you know that?"

"Believe me, the feeling's mutual."

He turned and was about to walk away from my doorstep when I stopped him. "Wait. Are you saying that you're not trying to manipulate me into giving in to your demands?"

"I'm only authorized to take certain lives. I don't have a lot of wiggle room in my contract."

I wanted to ask him more but he was gone. "Thanks for dropping by," I yelled into an empty street.

Great. Just great. I slammed the door of my house shut. I didn't know what to do. What did this mean? Had Arthur been telling me the truth? Or was this all part of some elaborate game? I supposed, so long as I stayed behind my wall of protection, there wasn't much he could do to me. Maybe he had to wait until I was out in the community and vulnerable.

But, as my outrage diminished, I started to wonder.

I was thinking about calling Diana, but we weren't exactly the best of friends like we had been even a week ago. I hesitated to involve her. And then to my surprise and shock my doorbell rang. I so rarely had visitors that I couldn't believe I'd get two in such a short time. Once more I peeped out through my peephole, and then with a cry of relief opened the door.

"Diana," I cried out, so happy to see her standing there.

"Thank goddess you're all right."

"Yes. But very relieved to see you."

"I had an instinct you were in trouble. I've brought you something."

"I'm so glad to see you. Please, come in."

She stepped in and then looked around the place, her nostrils quivering as she breathed in. "Something very bad has happened here. I smell burning."

"I told you. That's from the encounter I had with Arthur."

"You must cleanse this space. The energy in here is very bad."

"Not my first priority." And then I told her about Jane keeling over dead right in front of me. At book club.

"And you think Arthur killed her?"

I was so confused right now I didn't know what to believe.

"I did think so. I mean, don't you think it's a big coincidence? He tells me he's going to take me out with a brain aneurysm and then three days later a perfectly healthy woman falls on the floor dead. There's a doctor in our group. She said it was likely a brain aneurysm."

Diana pushed her silver hair back over her shoulder. "It could be a lot of things. I'm not a doctor, but what about a heart attack? What was the dead woman doing at the time?"

I thought back to those last few terrible moments of Jane's life. "She'd just taken a sip of her drink. Then she made a strange sound and stood up, took a couple of steps forward, and fell down on the floor dead."

"You and I know fifty substances that would cause someone to die like that."

A cold shiver went down my back. "What are you saying?"

"If I'd been there, I don't think I'd have suspected a brain aneurysm. I'd suspect poison."

"You mean Arthur might not have killed her?"

She said, "I think we need to look closer to home. I suspect that woman was murdered."

CHAPTER 4

efore she left, Diana pulled a package from her bag. It was a blue silk bag tied with ribbon, decorated with moons and stars. She said, "Put this under your pillow tonight. And pay attention to your dreams."

I took the bag in my hand and felt, it sounded crazy even to think it, but I felt like there was emotion coming from the bag. I couldn't have said what the emotion was, whether it was sadness or comfort. No, it was curiosity.

I looked at her and found her regarding me with sharp eyes. "You feel it, don't you?"

I nodded. "What's in this bag?"

"It's a special concoction all my own. One day I'll share it with you."

That's when I knew she was still angry with me. In the old days, she would have shared her secrets in a minute.

She reached out and touched my arm and then ran her fingers down until she wrapped the silver bracelet with her hand. Her fingers were strong and warm, and there was comfort there as well as strength. "Call me in the morning."

I nodded.

After she left, I locked the door and got out the sage and did a smudging ceremony to get rid of the negative energy. She was right. The air felt heavy and almost like I had to lift the negative energy physically before I could open the door and send it back out into the night.

That done, I drew a bath, chucking in lots of my own mixture of soothing oils and magic. I closed my eyes and leaned back, letting the scents soothe me and the water ease the stress from the muscles in my neck and upper back.

I thought about book club and that terrible moment when Jane had keeled over. Was it possible she'd been murdered?

Diana was right, though. I'd jumped so quickly to the conclusion that Arthur had killed Jane as a message to me or a punishment that I hadn't even considered other options. Besides, an actual medical doctor had jumped to conclusions too, so I couldn't be completely blamed for going along with her guess.

I suppose being a doctor, Maya would immediately go for the logical conclusion. How many people really got poisoned in their homes during a book club meeting? But we witches dealt less in science and hard facts and more in a less black and white world. No doubt, given the mysterious nature of her death, there would be some kind of investigation, probably an autopsy. That would tell us everything we needed to know. I just wondered how soon that would happen. In the meantime, I needed to know what had happened to her. I couldn't rest until I knew that Diana's version of events was the correct one, and my crazy idea that Arthur had somehow ended that woman's life prematurely was the wrong one.

And what if Jane had been poisoned? How would we find the culprit?

I didn't know why I felt this strong urge to interfere in what would no doubt be a police investigation, but I did.

And one thing I'd learned in forty-five years of trying to be a good witch was that I should never ignore my instincts.

I gazed at the candles flickering around the bathtub, a little vague through the steam of my bath. Maybe this was my chance to redeem myself from messing with death. Perhaps, if I could solve the mystery of Jane's murder, I could at least try to make that mistake right.

That made me feel better. I was getting sleepy, so I drained the bathtub, got out, and dried myself off with one of my big, fluffy towels. I got ready for bed and fetched the mysterious bag Diana had given me. I put it to my nose, trying to sniff out what was inside. There was lavender, and definitely rose petals, some spices, and...no. She'd thrown some stuff in there to fool me. I could open the bag and do a forensic investigation into its contents, but I decided not to. I trusted Diana, and she'd driven all the way out here to give me this.

The best thing I could do was slip it under my pillow and hope it gave me a really good night's sleep. I could certainly use one.

I needed to feel the comfort of people I loved and who loved me, so I dug out the pajamas my honorary nieces had bought me for Christmas. They were bright red flannel and had pictures of Scottie terriers all over them. They made me smile every time I looked at them and they were as warm as a hug when I put them on.

I had imagined that I would find it hard to sleep having so

recently witnessed a sudden death that was a possible murder. However, I tucked myself in, making sure the silk bag Diana had given me was well secured underneath my pillow. I breathed in and out a few times, conscious of the slight scent of lavender. What else did she put in there? As though I were cuddling a favorite stuffed animal, I rubbed my fingers against the silk bag. There were crystals in there for sure. A hardness that could be stone, shapes that could be twigs. Soft rain pattered on the rooftop and the sound soothed me to sleep.

I WAS WOKEN BY A CHILL. I opened my eyes and discovered I wasn't in my bed anymore. I was—I didn't know where I was. It was like a ruined castle with a stone floor and arches where the glass had long gone. There was no roof, just the ghostly remains of walls that seemed to reach up like bony fingers to the dark sky. The moon was partly obscured by heavy, dark clouds, and only a few stars pierced the gloom.

My feet were cold. I looked down and realized I was in bare feet. My bright red pajamas looked garish and out of place in this ancient ruin.

I had the sudden feeling that I wasn't alone and when I looked up again there was a man standing in front of me. He was all in black, in clothing that looked like something I'd have seen in an old black and white movie about swashbucklers.

He was holding a sword.

I waited for something to happen, but he just stood there regarding me. Finally, I asked, "Who are you?"

"I've been sent to collect you."

What was I, a recycling bin? Or old clothes to be donated to charity?

"I'm not a collectible." And that just made me think of all the kitschy things people collected. Cabbage Patch Dolls and Royal Doulton china ladies.

He chuckled softly. His voice was cool and British. "You are to my master."

The last guy who'd mysteriously appeared before me had worked for Death. I had a sinking feeling they both worked for the same guy.

"Did Arthur send you?"

He tapped the tip of his long, glinting sword against the stone near his booted foot. "Arthur passed your case on to me."

I was no more a case than I was a collectible. But I was definitely in trouble here.

I felt on my wrist for Diana's protection charm, but I'd taken the bracelet off when I had my bath. I'd forgotten to put it back on again.

However, I still had my innate skills.

Arthur had planned to knock me down with a brain aneurysm. This guy seemed a lot more old school. "What are you planning to do? Run me through with that thing?" Okay, I sounded sarcastic, but I was trembling from head to toe and it wasn't just from standing on cold stone.

"Your sister witch argued for you. We agreed to give you a fighting chance."

I was a middle-aged woman who'd never even been in a fistfight standing there in bare feet facing a guy holding what looked like a dueling sword. How was that a fighting chance?

As though he'd read my mind he said, "Look behind you."

I didn't want to turn my back on him, but he was standing at his ease, and I supposed being stabbed in the back wasn't much worse than being stabbed in the front. At least I wouldn't see it coming. So, I turned. On a stone step behind me was a dueling sword that looked identical to his and a pair of leather boots. I put the boots on first. Naturally they fit perfectly. I picked up the sword even though I had very little idea of what to do with it.

I turned and faced the man again. "This isn't exactly fair, you know. It's not like they taught fencing at South Seattle High."

"Pity."

"So, how does this work anyway?" I asked, bargaining for time. Surreptitiously I pinched myself. Maybe I would wake up from this nightmare and I'd be back in my comfy bed in Seattle. But, even though I'd pinched myself hard enough I'd leave a bruise, I remained in this cold, stone ruin facing a man who wanted to fight me to the death. "I can't kill you. All you're doing is dragging out the torture."

He shook his head. "We fight fair. You're right that you can't technically kill me, but if you run me through, you'll win your life back."

Oh, so simple. "Shouldn't I get like a handicap or something?" I don't know what I was thinking. This wasn't a golf tournament.

There was a sudden burst of thunder from the sky that made me jump. "And there's your answer," my companion said. He shifted until one booted foot was in front of the other, his right hand raised and his left hand held the deadly dueling sword pointed my way. "*En garde.*"

"Wait. I'm not ready." And I glanced up at the sky. "And you're being kind of dramatic, don't you think?"

"My master's impatient. We must begin."

"Or what?"

"My master will simply smite you down if you don't engage in this duel."

I supposed a creature who could cheer from the sidelines by invoking thunder and lightning was not somebody I really wanted to piss off. I grabbed my sword and held it up, hoping that desperation and the connection of all my witch sisters would guide my arm.

I muttered,

"Sisters mine, wherever you be,
Lend me your strength, lead me to victory.
Death would take me before my time.
Let me smite him before he commits that crime.
As I will, so mote it be."

And then I felt my arm strengthen and almost naturally seemed to find where to place my feet. As much as I really wished I'd thought to go to bed in leather breeches and a blousy, white shirt, I found myself standing there holding a sword in leather boots and bright red pajamas. With Scottie dogs all over them.

He moved towards me. Again, I had this insane notion that I'd somehow stumbled into an Errol Flynn picture. I moved backwards, but not fast enough, and our swords struck. The impact shuddered down my arm and, in spite of my witch's power, I didn't think this contest was going to last very long.

I could tell he was toying with me. Presumably if his master was watching this contest, he wanted to give him a little entertainment. And that just made me mad.

"I didn't mean to defy you," I yelled toward the moon. "You should give me another chance."

"This is your chance," my opponent said.

After that I didn't have time for any more arguing, I had to concentrate. I parried and thrust, and before tonight I wouldn't have known I could either parry or thrust. The steel in my arm felt like an extension of me somehow. I wasn't very good, but I stopped him from killing me two or three times. My problem was I didn't seem able to advance. My arm was already getting tired. I had to do something.

Maybe there was a witch around who could hear me? I yelled, "Help. Somebody help me."

This made the man in front of me chuckle. "We're quite remote, in case you hadn't noticed."

But my hearing was excellent. Wasn't that the thud of hoofbeats?

Maybe there was a witch on her way, or his way. Even the possibility of support gave me a burst of energy. I ran up the steps behind me in a move I'd definitely seen in a movie. He laughed, showing even, white teeth, and followed me up. Just like in the movies, I put my booted foot out to push him back down the stairs. Unlike in the movies, he grabbed my foot. I was about to go tumbling. If I didn't break my neck, he'd probably finish me off with that sword, when a new voice rang out.

"Unhand that lady."

CHAPTER 5

We both turned at the sound. Another man had appeared. He was tall, blond, and beautiful. Not a witch, I was certain, but the sweetest sight I could have imagined.

He wore clothes similar to the guy who was trying to kill me. But he was taller, broader. The moonlight caught a pale face and piercing blue eyes. He stripped off his cloak and gloves.

The guy trying to kill me dropped my foot. "This is none of your business, Lochlan Balfour."

"You mistake. You're on my land. I will not tolerate the murder of women." He pulled out his own sword.

Casually, the man in black trotted back down the stairs. "Go back to your realm, or face the consequences."

My favorite guy in the whole world laughed. Not an amused laugh. "I am undead. You hold no power over me."

Another clap of thunder came from on high, and, presumably taking the sound as guidance from his boss, the man in black rushed at the tall one he'd called Lochlan

Balfour. With the resuming of steel clashing against steel, the two fought with gusto. I'd never seen an honest-to-goodness duel in my life. It was elegant and raw and furious. Brutal and precise at the same time. Steel rang out and I could hear their boots brushing over the stone. I stretched my arm out, thankful for the rest, and sat on the stairs as though they were bleachers and I was watching a hockey game.

Wait a minute. What was I doing? I wasn't some damsel in distress who needed rescuing. Though yelling, 'Help, somebody please help me' at the top of my lungs could lead anyone into that error. The trouble was, if this big, blond hero was the one that dispatched Death's minion, he'd only send another one. I would have to end this fight on my own.

Reluctantly, I picked up my sword again and strode forward into battle.

The blond man saw me coming and held up his free hand. "Mistress, allow me to dispatch this mongrel cur."

"I'd love to, but I have to do it myself. If you kill him, they'll send another for me."

Steel rang on steel. It totally impressed me that he could carry on a conversation with me and still keep dueling with the guy in black.

"She's right," his opponent said, sweating freely and breathing heavily. The blond giant wasn't breathing heavily at all. He looked as though he could duel all day and then run a marathon.

Who was he?

He glanced at me, looking confused. "Have you the strength and skill to dispatch your aggressor?"

"No."

His eyes turned to me and glinted with sudden humor. "Then we have a problem."

Master of the understatement. "We do. Maybe you could coach me?" I said.

"While you're dueling?" he replied.

As though tired of this back and forth, the man in black suddenly lunged for me. It was during a moment of inattention when the man called Lochlan Balfour was looking at me, not him. I only caught the movement from the corner of my eye but I turned and, closing my eyes, shoved the dueling sword forward as hard as I could.

No one was more surprised than me when I felt the blade penetrate. Death's minion flailed away trying to get me even as he was falling. His sharp blade just nicked my wrist and then there was another clap of thunder and a bolt of lightning and he was gone in a puff of smoke.

My companion turned to me. "That was remarkably well done," he said admiringly.

I stretched my sword arm out. "Beginner's luck, believe me."

"Allow me to introduce myself. I am Lochlan Balfour." He made me a formal bow.

"I'm Quinn Callaghan. And I really appreciate you stopping by when you heard me yell for help."

"Mistress Callaghan, it was my pleasure." Then he came closer. His nostrils twitched and for a bad moment I felt something fierce and animalistic in him. He took a hasty step forward and then said, "You're bleeding."

I lifted my left hand and saw that he was right. There was a sharp slice on my wrist and blood was dripping from it.

Still, compared to being run through, I figured I'd got away pretty lightly.

"We must stop the bleeding," he said with suppressed intensity.

"It's just a flesh wound," I said. Never in my life would I have thought I would ever utter those words.

But he was already grabbing for a linen handkerchief, much larger than anything I'd ever seen. He bound it around my wrist, tying it tightly.

"And now I must leave you." He still seemed kind of fidgety, which was weird when he'd been so calm before.

"Okay. Thanks again." Before he left, he picked up my right hand in his and kissed it.

"I hope we meet again."

Unless I time traveled, I really doubted it. Still, it seemed rude not to say, "Me too."

And then he strode out. A minute later I heard the sound of horse's hooves galloping away.

I stood there, alone in a ruined castle wondering what on earth to do.

I looked up, held my hands wide. "Okay. Show's over."

A clap of thunder made me jump. I opened my eyes. I had that strange feeling where I didn't know where I was. My room felt foreign. I looked instinctively for the clock radio beside my bed and the digital numbers glowed 5:14. I groaned and snuggled back down in my comfy bed. Somehow the cover had got tossed off me and I felt cold. I always slept with my window slightly open and a storm had obviously kicked up in the night. I felt too lazy to get up and shut the window, so I just pulled the quilt higher and drifted back to sleep.

I TOOK a while to wake up. It was still very early, but I was done with sleep. I got up and padded to the kitchen to put the coffee on. I'd had the weirdest dream in the night. It was one of those that was still kind of fuzzy and I should write down the details before I forgot it. I reached to put on the coffee pot and as I did, I felt a twinge in my left wrist. Still groggy from sleep, I looked down and noticed a handkerchief tied around my wrist. I could see the rustiness where a little blood had soaked through. And as I stood there, my whole body went cold. The 'dream' came back to me like a freezing wave of water right in my face.

Not a dream. If I had bled, then in some fashion I had actually been in that ruin of a castle fighting, who exactly? One of Death's employees? I had fought for my life. And then that gorgeous blond who looked like a Viking with ice blue eyes and blond hair had quite literally ridden to my rescue. I recalled the sound of the pounding hooves and the courtly way he'd tried to save my life. This was his handkerchief wrapped around my wrist. I touched it gingerly. I didn't think we'd been in present day, but probably we'd been in some kind of realm where time was fluid.

I had to get to work, but I also needed to take a moment and write down what I remembered. I went upstairs to clean my wound and shower. When I went to make my bed, a tail of ribbon peeking from under the pillow caught my attention, and then hot fury washed through me. Diana. Diana and her sachet that was supposed to give me what? Good dreams? She had to be in on this. Was she working with Death to get rid of me?

The woman had been my friend. Now something else came back to me. The guy fighting me had told me that my sister had negotiated me a fighting chance. Diana had to have known she was sending me to my death.

I didn't know what to do, I was so angry. Well, I decided I wouldn't do anything for now. I'd go to work as usual. It wasn't easy to keep my focus, but I did my best. Being a law librarian is mostly research, and no one needed anything pressing so I could go through the motions of doing my job while my brain was elsewhere.

Around ten in the morning I got a text from Diana. "How are you?"

Seriously?

I ignored her for an hour, and then I wrote back, "Not dead. Surprised?" And then I turned my phone off.

CHAPTER 6

I turned my phone back on at the end of the day and had a number of messages. Three calls from Diana, which I ignored, and one from Jane Eddington's husband. I called him back wondering if there was any news on his wife's death, but surprisingly he told me how much book club had meant to Jane and he wanted each of us to choose a keepsake. "I thought perhaps you might like one of the books from her extensive library."

Based on Jane Eddington's reading tastes, I was pretty sure I didn't want anything out of her library. But I appreciated the thoughtfulness.

"Have they told you anything about how she died?" I asked.

"No. They're still doing tests. I don't know what that means. She obviously had a heart attack or aneurysm or something. I'm not sure what the holdup is."

I thought maybe I did. I told him I'd take care of getting the other book club members together and thanked him. I was reliving those moments when she had keeled over and I began to wonder about the husband. The way she'd been so domineering over her book club made me wonder what she'd been like to be married to. Had the henpecked husband finally had enough?

I was pondering death as I walked up the leafy street to my house. Evening was drawing in and I didn't notice the figure standing beneath a tree on the sidewalk in front until it stepped forward. I nearly jumped out of my skin.

"Quinn Callahan. I didn't mean to startle you."

If seeing a man move unexpectedly had startled me, recognizing him pretty much poleaxed me. I had seen this man very recently, but in my dreams. It was the tall, blond man who'd come when I'd called for help.

"Lochlan Balfour?" I asked in a voice that trembled.

"No need to be afraid. I won't harm you."

"Are you real?" I slapped my face to see if I was awake, but I definitely was. "Ouch. Last time I saw you, I was dreaming."

He raised his hand and did a back-and-forth movement with it. "Not exactly. Our notions of time and reality are somewhat different."

"But you were wearing clothes from, I don't know, hundreds of years ago."

"I am older than I appear."

I thought back to what he'd said last night. "Are you undead?"

"Does that frighten you?"

I was a witch. Who was I to be frightened of a vampire? And then I recalled the way he'd acted when blood had been dripping from my wrist. No wonder he'd suddenly gone twitchy. I must have smelled like dinner. I had to give him credit, he hadn't stayed around to enjoy a full meal. He'd taken off pretty quickly. Instinctively I glanced at my wrist, but the wound was already closed up and scabbing over.

He followed my gaze and smiled slightly. "You're safe with me. The current time is much simpler for people of my persuasion."

I was puzzled for a moment and then nodded. "Right. Medical advances. Blood banks."

"Exactly."

For what seemed like the hundredth time in a few days, I asked a man, "What are you doing here?"

I really, really hoped he wasn't out to kill me, because I didn't have much fight left.

"I was worried about you. I'm not sure I did you any favors helping to fight on your behalf. I was a mortal in the time of chivalry. It's a hard habit to break."

"Please, don't ever break it on my behalf. You did save me. If you hadn't given me a rest and then helped kill that guy, I'd be finished."

"You killed the creature who'd been sent to fight you to the death."

But there was still a worried looking frown between his eyebrows.

"Do you think he's going to come after me again?"

"Death isn't the most generous of adversaries. With your permission, I'll remain in the background until it's clear that you're safe."

"Why would you do that? You don't even know me."

He shook his head. "In my long existence, I've discovered that we are more connected than we think."

I glanced up and down the street, but apart from a dog walker a block away, there didn't seem to be anyone about.

"It's getting cold out here. Why don't you come inside and we'll talk about it some more."

"It's very generous of you to invite me into your home." And then I remembered that bit of folklore that vampires couldn't enter unless you invited them. I stood my ground.

"You're not going to make a meal of me, are you?"

He drew himself up to a full, impressive height and looked at me quite frostily. "I am a man of my word."

"Come on then."

I unlocked the door and let him in. I didn't really know what the correct protocol was when entertaining a vampire. "Would you like a seat?"

"Thank you."

I switched on a lamp and took him into the living room where he waited until I was seated before sitting down himself. Such manners. He wore designer jeans and a tweed jacket over a black t-shirt. He looked like a very sexy Seattle business guy. He looked like a Viking, but his accent was somewhere from the British Isles.

"Where are you from?" I asked him.

"Ireland originally. And I have business interests there still. I spend a good deal of my time in Ireland. But also here. I'm involved in technology so I often find myself in Seattle."

My eyes widened. "You're that Lochlan Balfour?"

"I am."

Lochlan Balfour had founded a tech start-up that had earned him a few billion. His company provided internet security among other things, but, while his name was well known, he was notoriously reclusive. Now I knew why.

"Look, it's been a really stressful day. I'm opening a bottle of red wine. Can I offer you a glass?"

"I'd be very grateful."

Okay, so he drank red wine. I didn't wish to pry but if he wanted anything else, he was going to have to let me know.

I got the wine, and on instinct went with one of my nicer bottles. A guy who dressed like that had to be used to the finer things in life.

"To your good health," I said raising my glass.

"And to yours," he said, a shaft of humor lighting his eyes.

Right. My health was a lot more precarious right now since it was attached to my life. He, on the other hand, was fairly bulletproof.

He stretched out his long legs and regarded me. "May I ask what you did to anger Death?"

Weirdly, it was nice to be able to share my story with someone who didn't know me at all. Somebody I could count on in a tight spot. Besides, he seemed genuinely interested, and so I told him everything. How I'd tried to extend my ex-husband's life using magic, how my coven was now mad at me, and that I wasn't sure if I was out of the woods yet.

My phone signaled an incoming text and I saw one from Maya, the doctor who was in our book club. It said, *We should find a time when we can all meet to honor Jane.*

"What is it?" Lochlan asked, watching my face. "You look troubled."

Oh, what the hell. I'd told him everything else, why not this?

"A woman died in front of me at our book club." Then I hesitated. "You probably don't even know what a book club is."

Once again that wintery amusement crossed his face. "I

do. I'm in a book club myself, in fact. In the town of Bally-dehag in Ireland."

And look at me rushing to judgment. "I apologize. Well, one of our book club members dropped dead in her home during book club. I think she might have been poisoned. And I'm pretty sure either her husband, or one of the other book club members, is the culprit."

I hadn't thought of him as particularly relaxed, but now I could see that he had been because he went so alert. "Describe her death." When I raised my eyebrows at him, he said, "I've seen many." Winced slightly. "Caused a few."

So didn't want to go there. I described exactly what I'd seen, as much as I could remember it.

"It does sound like poison. But it could have been an allergy. A natural poison, too. Did she ingest food or drink?"

I gasped. "The mushrooms."

He nodded slowly. "There are many a deadly mushroom that one must be wary of."

"One of the women was so proud. She brought polenta with wild mushrooms and she told us she'd sourced them herself." I stared at him. "Could that be it?"

"Certainly. But, wouldn't that be an accidental poisoning?"

I felt so relieved. "It would. And then I wouldn't need to worry that one of my friends was a murderer."

"And she was the only one who ate the mushrooms?"

And there went that theory crashing to the floor like a delicate crystal glass shattering. I shook my head. "I ate the mushrooms and nothing happened to me."

He said, "If your friend was poisoned, it had to be something that the murderer knew only she would ingest. Or they had access to her food or drink or medicines."

"Her husband would." I didn't even know if the woman had been on any medications. And then it hit me with a gasp. "The scotch."

"Scotch whiskey?"

"We all drank wine, but Jane Eddington only ever drank scotch. And she kept it in a cut crystal decanter." I looked at him. "Do you think that's how she was killed?"

"I think it would be an excellent idea to test the contents of that decanter."

"But that won't narrow down who did it."

"No. For that, you would need to set a trap."

"Yes," I said, suddenly filled with energy and resolve. "Yes, a trap is exactly what we need, and I think I know how to do it."

I told him that Jane's husband had invited each of us to go to the house and choose a book to remember Jane by. "What if I suggest we meet there all together one last time? I'm sure her husband would go for it. Then I'll suggest that we all toast Jane with her own scotch." I was really warming to this idea. "And we'll know who the murderer is, because they'll be the one who refuses to drink."

"Unless they've already disposed of the poisoned scotch."

What a buzz kill. "It's not a perfect plan, but it's all I've got."

"Who do you think is the most likely killer?"

"None of them. These are all my friends."

"Tell me about these people and what you know of their relationship with the woman who died."

I marshaled my thoughts. "She's been married to Ronald

for"—I did some quick math—"it must be forty years. He looked a little frightened of her, but I think they were happy enough."

"Many an unhappy spouse makes away with the other through secretive means. Let us not discount the husband. Go on."

"Maya is a medical doctor. She's been coming to the book club longer than I have, and I've been a member for seven years. They're neighbors." I swallowed. "It was Maya who said she suspected a brain aneurysm. And it was also Maya who foraged for the mushrooms."

He sat silent, listened carefully, and I could tell he was sifting through the details. He said, "But you stated that Jane wasn't the only one who ate the mushrooms. You ate them yourself."

"Yes," I replied, leaning forward. "But remember, she's a doctor. What if she had one lethal mushroom among the benign ones and made sure that Jane got it. It would look like an accident. Happens every year. Mushroom foragers mistaking poisonous mushrooms for tasty ones."

"But why would she kill her friend?"

"I don't know."

"Who else was there?"

"Kanako brought the sushi. She's a graphic artist in her late fifties, early sixties. I think she was brought into the group by Maya. They're friends."

"Can you think of any reason why she would want to kill Jane Eddington?"

"No more than any of us wanted to kill Jane." And then I remembered one thing. "After we all left the house that night, she went back. She said she'd forgotten her phone, which was probably true given that we were pretty shaken up. And she'd been the one who called 911, so she could have accidentally left her phone on the floor."

"Or, she could have been going back to get rid of the poison."

Which would pretty much take the spring out of our trap.

"Who else?"

"Frances has known Ronald and Jane longer than any of us. She and Jane worked together at the university. Jane was her boss. Even now that they're presumably equals, two retired university professors, Jane treats her like a subordinate."

"You say she's known the pair of them a long time? Is she a married woman?"

"I'm not sure she ever married."

"Perhaps there's something worth exploring there? Does she seem overly fond of the husband, perhaps?"

I tried to look back at previous book club meetings through suspicious eyes, but Ronald had never been allowed to join in our actual discussion. He was always putting the food out and topping up wine. I shook my head. "Kanako is usually the one who helps Ronald with the food. If anybody had a crush on him, I would have said it was her. And she's divorced."

His eyes were sharp on mine. "And she returned to the house."

"The only other person in book club is Kimberlee. She's in her twenties and in awe of Jane. She's working on her PhD. I can't imagine why she might want to kill her mentor."

"Students can be very sensitive. If this woman is as harsh

as you say she is, perhaps she said unkind things about her protégée's thesis?"

Oh, he was good. I hadn't even thought of this. But Jane did seem like the kind of person who would choose to be harsh and honest over diplomatic.

"And then there's me. I originally thought it was my fault she was dead, because I thought Arthur was interfering, but he swears he didn't, which means I had nothing to do with her death."

"I am very glad to hear it."

Suddenly, I was filled with determination. Maybe I was trying to balance the wrong I'd done in extending my ex-husband's life by solving an innocent woman's murder. Whatever the reason, I felt driven to figure out what had happened.

"We need a plan," I said. "I can't serve poisoned scotch. The murderer won't drink it, but how am I going to stop anybody else knocking it back? I don't want to kill the rest of book club."

"No. You cannot put others at risk that way. You must replace it with a decanter just like it."

"But how am I going to do that?"

"I will take care of that part for you." He smiled thinly. "I'll be in and out before anyone knows I've been there."

"So, it's an old wives' tale that you have to be invited to cross the threshold?"

He shook his head and closed his eyes with an expression of fastidious loathing. "The nonsense people make up about my kind."

"Right."

Fortunately, I knew exactly what the decanter looked like because Jane often raved about her antique Waterford crystal.

The decanter was from the Lismore pattern, and with a little online searching I found one for sale at an antique store nearby. "Look, here it is. Lismore spirit decanter. That's exactly the same as Jane's."

"Excellent work," he said, looking over my shoulder.

"We'll have to wait till tomorrow during business hours to pick it up," I said.

He looked at me like I wasn't the sparkliest crystal in the set. "Please. Just give me the address."

My jaw fell open. "You're going to steal it?"

"I'll look at the tag and deposit the money in the till if it makes you feel better."

"Much better. Thanks."

I glanced up at him. "You couldn't also pick me up a bottle of Glenfiddich, could you?"

"Consider it done." He said, "I have extensive contacts, as you might imagine. I'll make sure to get the original scotch tested. I'll also need this Jane Eddington's address." He pulled out a much fancier cell phone than mine and we exchanged phone numbers. What a modern vampire he was.

He rose to leave. "I'll call you in the morning."

"You're going now?"

He smiled at me a little. "I do my best work at night. That part isn't a myth."

CHAPTER 7

As soon as Lochlan Balfour left, I got on the phone. Ronald sounded grateful when I suggested the group all get together at his place the next evening. He'd been the one I'd been worried about, but he was an enthusiastic supporter of an impromptu book club get-together at Jane's house to honor her and say goodbye.

After that was easy. I phoned the rest of the book club and if they had plans for the next evening, they said they'd change them. We agreed to meet at seven at night. Our usual meeting time.

I was nervous. What if I was wrong? What if Jane hadn't died that way? And the killer somehow got away with murder?

Or maybe she actually had had a heart attack or brain aneurysm. Whatever the police knew, they weren't saying. There'd been an obituary in today's paper and that was it.

I headed to Jane Eddington's house fifteen minutes early. Lochlan had called earlier and assured me he'd swapped the decanters and made sure the level of scotch was exactly the same as it had been. That was a relief. I still wanted to get there early just to feel the atmosphere and make sure I knew where the scotch glasses were.

As I walked up the walk to the front door, I happened to glance in the dining-room window and there was Ronald. With him was Kanako. They weren't embracing, but the way they looked at each other said everything. My jaw dropped. It wasn't Frances who'd been in love with Ronald Eddington. It was Kanako. Kanako, who had run back in after we'd all left. To comfort her lover? Or to get rid of the evidence that she'd murdered his wife?

I gave them a few moments to move away from the window, and then I knocked on the door.

Ronald opened it, looking somewhat surprised. "Quinn. Thank you for coming. Are you early or am I late?"

"I'm early. I wondered how you're doing?"

"Aren't you kind?" He opened the door, and I stepped inside. Kanako came walking out of the dining room.

"You're so sweet, Quinn," she said, tucking a loose strand of hair behind her ear. "I came on the same errand. I thought Ronald might need someone to talk to."

Ronald looked as though he didn't know what to do. "Would you like to choose one of Jane's books now? I know she'd have wanted you all to have something of hers."

Kanako and I exchanged a glance. She looked at me with blank friendliness, but my brain was seething. Was I looking right at a murderer?

I said, "Why don't we wait until everybody's here?"

"Fine. Fine." He led us into the living room where we always had our meetings and the three of us settled awkwardly. I went instinctively to the yellow velvet chair I'd sat in at our last meeting, and Kanako took a seat on the couch. Ronald sat on the opposite side of the room. Jane's favorite chair remained empty.

Luckily, the other women were prompt. And before Ronald could get everybody in her library looking at books, I raised my voice. "Could we gather in the living room for a minute? I thought we'd say a few words about our friend Jane."

Who was going to argue with that? Everyone trooped into the living room and sat down.

My heart was hammering away in my chest, but I managed to keep my voice level.

Since it had been my idea to say a few words, they naturally all looked at me. Ronald stood up and said, "You won't want me here. I'll head into the kitchen and put some coffee on."

"No," I stopped him. "Please. We'd like you to stay."

Going slightly pink, he resumed his seat.

I said, "I know Jane's left us, but I thought we'd go around the room and each share a little memory of her. But first, I think we should have a toast."

I went to the glass-fronted cabinet where she kept her crystal and opened it. I began taking out tumblers and putting them in front of each person.

"What are you doing?" Kimberlee asked.

"We're going to toast Jane with her favorite scotch." I spoke with such determination that no one argued. So far, so good. When I had crystal tumblers in front of everybody, I picked up the decanter. Lochlan had done a perfect job. I even knew it had been replaced and it looked exactly the same to me. I went around and splashed a generous couple of fingers into each glass.

No one picked it up. Maya eyed the scotch and then glanced up at me with distaste. "I've never been a scotch drinker."

"It's for Jane," I said. "Wherever you are, Jane, your story ended far too soon. Tonight we salute you," and I raised my glass and said, "To Jane," and then I looked around.

"To Jane," everyone echoed. It seemed like slow motion as I watched hands move glasses closer to lips. Would the murderer risk poisoning us all?

I looked at Kanako. She was staring at the scotch as though she wanted to throw it across the room. Tears filled her eyes.

Kimberlee sniffed her drink as though she'd never tasted scotch before. Or was she sniffing to detect whether the poison was still in the decanter?

Maya had her face squinched up in distaste, clearly waiting for the rest of us to go first.

Ronald gazed at the glass in his hand and tears streamed down his face.

Maybe I'd been wrong. I put the glass against my lower lip. The peaty scotch scent was in my nostrils and I was about to drink, a sound rent the air.

"No. Stop."

Frances jumped to her feet. She was red in the face. "Put the glasses down. Put them down."

Maya, ever the doctor, stood up and took a step towards her friend, who looked like she was having some kind of fit.

"Frances, what's wrong?"

The woman collapsed to the couch, tears running down

her face. "I just couldn't stand it anymore. That scotch is poisoned. You must throw it away. If you drink it, you'll die."

In the general gasps and exclamations of disbelief, I made myself heard. "Why Frances? Why did you kill Jane Eddington?"

It was like the answer was flung from the deepest part of her soul. "You don't know what it was like! Forty years I worked with that woman. I was her best friend. And all she ever did was belittle and humiliate me. She never even let me choose a book for book club." She was red in the face and stood up. "I couldn't take it anymore. I said to myself I would give her one more chance. If she let me choose just one story for us to read, I would let her live. But she couldn't do that. She couldn't even give me that. So, I poisoned her scotch."

She glanced around at all of us and hiccupped a sob. "But I never meant any of you any harm. Or you, Ronald. Now at least you can be free to marry Kanako."

Kanako and Ronald glanced at each other and then at Frances, looking horrified. "How did you know?"

"I caught you once, kissing in the kitchen. I never would have said anything. I was just glad that Ronald could be happy finally. But in a way it was worse. Before he fell in love with you, I always knew that he was as miserable as I was. And then when I saw you two together, I knew he wasn't unhappy anymore. It was just me. And so I did what I had to do."

I had wondered if she might try to run for it, but instead she said, "I'll go to prison, of course. May I take one of her books with me to remember her by?"

Ronald didn't seem to know what to say and then finally just nodded.

49

While she was choosing her book, the police arrived.

Maya looked at me. "You set this up!"

There was no point pretending I hadn't. Soon I'd tell the police everything. So, I nodded.

"You took a terrible risk. What if one of us had sipped the scotch and died? That would have been your fault."

I shook my head. "No. It wouldn't. You can drink that scotch. I hid the real one away." And then I walked over to the cupboard where I'd told Lochlan to hide the poisoned drink, opened it, and pointed. "It's in there."

She calmed down then. "I'm sorry she died like that. But I'm glad you solved her murder."

I was, too.

Much later, I left Jane Eddington's house for the last time. I had a novel of hers tucked into my bag. Jane Austen. One of my favorites, and a novel that ended happily. I liked to think that in spite of her passion for death, despair, and madness, Jane could sometimes allow for the possibility of a happy ending.

But would I get mine?

I hadn't gone far when Lochlan Balfour materialized beside me, as I had somehow known he would.

"It all went exactly according to plan," I told him. When I told him Frances had killed her oldest friend, he didn't look very surprised. "How did you know it was her?"

"I didn't. But, one thing I do know about murder is that it's rarely sudden. That kind of anger can take years to grow."

I supposed in all his centuries on the earth he'd developed quite a bit of wisdom about human nature.

"Will you stay around?" I asked him. He seemed like a handy guy to know.

He shook his head. "My business here will be done very soon."

"I'm sorry to hear that. It's been nice getting to know you."

He smiled down at me. "Oh, we'll be seeing each other again. Your coven sisters will want to be the ones to tell you, but the head of your coven—Diana, is it?—and Death made a deal. You must leave this place. You're being banished to Ireland."

I stopped walking and had to hold onto a handy fence. "Banished? To Ireland?"

"To a small town named Ballydehag. I live there."

I would throw fits and argue myself hoarse before I agreed to this. But I didn't tell Lochlan I was never moving to some no-account town in Ireland. All I said was, "Well, we'll have lots to talk about."

He looked down at me, sadly. He put his hand out and cupped the back of my head. Raised my chin with his other hand. I thought for a second he was going to kiss me, but he said, "Unfortunately, you'll have no memory of our encounter."

I was so stunned I stared into those icy blue eyes.

"But we will see each other again."

Thanks for reading *Crossing the Lines.* I hope you enjoyed Quinn's adventure. Keep reading for a sneak peek of book 1 in the Vampire Book Club series.

The Vampire Book Club, Chapter 1

HAVE you ever wondered what your life would be like if you'd made one crucial decision differently? What if you hadn't married that man that everyone said was perfect? If you'd taken the job you wanted instead of that one with the good medical benefits? What if you'd moved to New York after college instead of Seattle?

I used to imagine what would have happened if I'd taken the other path. Maybe not the road less traveled, just not traveled by me. It was a harmless exercise to pass the time while I toiled at my boring job, safe from any threat of change.

Until one day I messed with fate.

And I was punished.

I got change all right. More than I could have imagined. My staid life was uprooted. My road was forked. Frankly, I was forked.

At forty-five, I was both divorced and widowed (from the same man), I lost the secure but dull job I'd had for ten years, and the powers that be sent me across the sea to Ireland.

It all happened so fast, my head was still spinning when my Aer Lingus flight from Seattle landed in Dublin. From there, I took a train to Cork. It was early May, and as I looked out the window, I began to realize why they called Ireland the Emerald Isle. It was so vibrantly green, and between fields of cows and sheep, ruined castles and cottages, we stopped at pretty-sounding towns and cities to let passengers on and off. I smiled when we passed through Limerick and started making up rhymes in my head. They weren't very good, but they passed the time.

There once was a misguided witch
Who tried a man's fate to switch
Her punishment set
To Ireland she must get
But better than feathers and pitch!

From Cork city, I got a bus, though I vowed to come back and explore the pretty city when I was settled. Finally, jet-lagged and travel-weary, I arrived in my new home. The town of Ballydehag.

The bus let me off in front of Finnegan's Grocery. As the curly-haired driver retrieved my two heavy suitcases from the storage compartment underneath the bus, I thanked him. He replied, "Good luck to you, ma'am."

There's a way of wishing a person luck that sounds like you actually wish them good things, and then there's a way of wishing a person good luck that sounds more like, "What on earth have you done?"

I was wondering what on earth I'd done, too, but I was here, now. I pulled my phone out with the address of my new home and then stared vaguely about me. I had no idea where I was, except that this was clearly the main street of a pretty Irish village. The street was lined with shops. A couple of old men in caps sat outside a coffee shop regarding me. I wondered if the arrival of the bus from Cork was a big event. And didn't that say a lot about how exciting this town was?

I couldn't think of anything else to do but go into Finnegan's and hope whoever worked there might know Rose Cottage.

I didn't think my suitcases would even fit through the narrow front door of the shop, and besides, this didn't look like much of a high-crime area, so I pushed my two cases up against the white plaster wall and walked in.

It was like stepping into the past. Narrow rows with shelves of groceries stretched from ceiling to floor and seemed to contain everything from eggs to pest-control products.

I heard voices and turned to the right and the only checkout. A plump woman with curly gray hair stood behind the counter. She wore a green cardigan with the sleeves rolled up her wrists and all the mother-of-pearl buttons done up. The edge of the sweater was scalloped, and the collar of a crisp, white blouse framed her face. She was gossiping with two customers who stood on the opposite side of the counter. "Hello?" I interrupted.

The three stopped talking and all turned to stare at me. I smiled brightly and tried to look nonthreatening. "I'm wondering if you can help me. Do you have the number of a taxi?"

They all looked at each other as though they had never heard the word taxi before. "A taxicab?" I tried again. "I'm trying to get to a place called Rose Cottage. Do you know where that is?"

The man, tall and thin with pale blue eyes, looked as though a great puzzle had been solved. "Rose Cottage. Ah." He nodded. The other two nodded as well.

There was silence. Me again? "Could you direct me to Rose Cottage? I have two suitcases outside. I was hoping to get a cab to take me there."

The man scratched his head. "I could fetch me wheelbarrow."

The woman behind the counter shook her head at him.

"A wheelbarrow. Honestly. I can drive you around, love. It's not far. Danny, you come and stand behind this counter, and if anyone wants to buy anything, you just write down what it is, or they can wait until I get back. I won't be a minute."

Was this woman actually going to leave her post to drive a complete stranger? "I don't want to take you away from your work," I stammered.

"Oh, it's no trouble. And you've chosen a good time. We're not very busy."

Danny looked quite pleased to walk behind the counter and stand there very importantly. He began tidying up open packs of chocolate bars as though he owned the place.

"I'm Kathleen McGinnis," said the woman who'd come from behind the cash desk. I warmed to her immediately, but I'd warm to anyone who was willing to drive me to my new home. "And you must be Quinn Callahan."

I did a double take. "You knew I was coming?"

"I've been on the lookout for you."

Read the rest of the *Vampire Book Club*, book 1 in the Vampire Book Club series.

A Note from Nancy

Dear Reader,

Thank you for reading *Crossing the Lines*, the Vampire Book Club prequel. I hope you'll consider leaving a review and please tell your friends who paranormal women's fiction and cozy mysteries.

You can review *Crossing the Lines* on Amazon, Goodreads or BookBub.

Don't let the fun end. Let's stay in touch.

Join my newsletter for a free prequel, *Tangles and Treason*, the exciting tale of how the gorgeous Rafe Crosyer, from The Vampire Knitting Club series, was turned into a vampire.

I hope to see you in my private Facebook Group *Nancy Warren's Knitwits* where the fun continues daily.

Until next time,
Happy Reading,

Nancy

ALSO BY NANCY WARREN

The best way to keep up with new releases, plus enjoy bonus content and prizes is to join Nancy's newsletter at NancyWarrenAuthor.com or join her in her private FaceBook group Nancy Warren's Knitwits.

~

Vampire Knitting Club: Paranormal Cozy Mystery

Lucy Swift inherits an Oxford knitting shop and the late-night knitting club of vampires who live downstairs.

Tangles and Treason - A free ebook for newsletter subscribers. A paperback version is available for sale. NancyWarrenAuthor.com

Ribbing and Runes - Book 13

Mosaics and Magic - Book 14

Cables and Conjurers - Book 15

Cat's Paws and Curses - A Holiday Whodunnit

Vampire Knitting Club Mega Paperback Series Bundle

Vampire Knitting Club Boxed Set: Books 1-3

Vampire Knitting Club Boxed Set: Books 4-6

Vampire Knitting Club Boxed Set: Books 7-9

Vampire Knitting Club Boxed Set: Books 10-12

Vampire Knitting Club Ebook Boxed Set: Books 13-15

LARGE PRINT EDITIONS: Vampire Knitting Club

Available in paperback or hardback large print format.

Tangles and Treason - Prequel.

The Vampire Knitting Club - Book 1

Stitches and Witches - Book 2

Crochet and Cauldrons - Book 3

Vampire Knitting Club: Cornwall: Paranormal Cozy Mystery

Boston-bred witch Jennifer Cunningham agrees to run a knitting
and yarn shop in a fishing village in Cornwall, England—with
characters from the Oxford-set *Vampire Knitting Club* series.

The Vampire Knitting Club: Cornwall - Book 1

Scallops and Sorcerers - Book 2

Village Flower Shop: Paranormal Cozy Mystery

In a picture-perfect Cotswold village, flowers, witches, and murder
make quite the bouquet for flower shop owner Peony Bellefleur.

Peony Dreadful - Book 1

Karma Camellia - Book 2

Highway to Hellebore - Book 3

Luck of the Iris - Book 4

Game of Thorns - Book 5

Vampire Book Club: Paranormal Women's Fiction Cozy Mystery

Seattle witch Quinn Callahan's midlife crisis is interrupted when she gets sent to Ballydehag, Ireland, to run an unusual bookshop.

Crossing the Lines - Prequel

The Vampire Book Club - Book 1

Chapter and Curse - Book 2

A Spelling Mistake - Book 3

A Poisonous Review - Book 4

In Want of a Knife - Book 5

Vampire Book Club Boxed Set: Books 1-3

Great Witches Baking Show: Paranormal Culinary Cozy Mystery

Poppy Wilkinson, an American with English roots, joins a reality show to win the crown of Britain's Best Baker—and to get inside Broomewode Hall to uncover the secrets of her past.

The Great Witches Baking Show - Book 1

Baker's Coven - Book 2

A Rolling Scone - Book 3

A Bundt Instrument - Book 4

Blood, Sweat and Tiers - Book 5

Crumbs and Misdemeanors - Book 6

A Cream of Passion - Book 7

Cakes and Pains - Book 8

Whisk and Reward - Book 9

Gingerdead House - A Holiday Whodunnit

The Great Witches Baking Show Boxed Set: Books 1-3

The Great Witches Baking Show Boxed Set: Books 4-6 (includes bonus novella)

The Great Witches Baking Show Boxed Set: Books 7-9

Abigail Dixon: 1920s Cozy Historical Mystery

In 1920s Paris everything is très chic, except murder.

Murder at the Paris Fashion House - Book 1

Death at Darrington Manor - Book 2

Toni Diamond Mysteries

Toni Diamond is a successful saleswoman for Lady Bianca Cosmetics in this series of humorous cozy mysteries.

Frosted Shadow - Book 1

Ultimate Concealer - Book 2

Midnight Shimmer - Book 3

A Diamond Choker For Christmas - A Holiday Whodunnit

Toni Diamond Mysteries Boxed Set: Books 1-4

The Almost Wives Club: Contemporary Romantic Comedy

An enchanted wedding dress is a matchmaker in this series of romantic comedies where five runaway brides find out who the best men really are.

The Almost Wives Club: Kate - Book 1

Secondhand Bride - Book 2

Bridesmaid for Hire - Book 3

The Wedding Flight - Book 4

If the Dress Fits - Book 5

The Almost Wives Club Boxed Set: Books 1-5

Take a Chance: Contemporary Romance

Meet the Chance family, a cobbled together family of eleven kids who are all grown up and finding their ways in life and love.

Chance Encounter - Prequel

Kiss a Girl in the Rain - Book 1

Iris in Bloom - Book 2

Blueprint for a Kiss - Book 3

Every Rose - Book 4

Love to Go - Book 5

The Sheriff's Sweet Surrender - Book 6

The Daisy Game - Book 7

Take a Chance Boxed Set: Prequel and Books 1-3

For a complete list of books, check out Nancy's website at NancyWarrenAuthor.com

ABOUT THE AUTHOR

Nancy Warren is the USA Today Bestselling author of more than 100 novels. She's originally from Vancouver, Canada, though she tends to wander and has lived in England, Italy, and California at various times. While living in Oxford she dreamed up The Vampire Knitting Club. Favorite moments include being the answer to a crossword puzzle clue in Canada's National Post newspaper, being featured on the front page of the New York Times when her book *Speed Dating* launched Harlequin's NASCAR series, and being nominated three times for Romance Writers of America's RITA award. She has an MA in Creative Writing from Bath Spa University. She's an avid hiker, loves chocolate, and most of all, loves to hear from readers!

The best way to stay in touch is to sign up for Nancy's newsletter at NancyWarrenAuthor.com or www.facebook.com/groups/NancyWarrenKnitwits

To learn more about Nancy and her books
NancyWarrenAuthor.com

facebook.com/AuthorNancyWarren

x.com/nancywarren1

instagram.com/nancywarrenauthor

amazon.com/Nancy-Warren/e/B001H6NM5Q

goodreads.com/nancywarren

bookbub.com/authors/nancy-warren

www.ingramcontent.com/pod-product-compliance
Lightning Source LLC
Chambersburg PA
CBHW071203130626
46555CB00004B/1563